First published 2018
by Rowanvale Books Ltd
The Gate
Keppoch Street
Roath
Cardiff
CF24 3JW
www.rowanvalebooks.com
Library Cataloguing in Publication Data.
A catalogue record for this book is available from the British Library.

*This book is dedicated to my mum, Marjorie Vanston (19.9.25 - 1.12.17)
who loved this poem and liked to read it aloud every Christmas.*

On Christmas Eve, as Santa sat
To put on boots and coat and hat,
All the reindeer stood around
And waited there without a sound

To take the present-laden sleigh –
Which looked amazing, by the way –
To all good children and deliver
Presents from the present-giver.

But nothing happened, not that night,
Though all was clear, and all was bright,
Conditions perfect for a sleigh
To be on time for Christmas Day,
As reindeer waited in the snow,
Santa said: "Please, wait a mo."

For on that soft and silent night
Something just was not quite right.
Then Santa stood and gave a sigh,
No glint or sparkle in his eye,
"I'm sorry," he said, "I've done my best –
I've got to get this off my chest."

The silent, falling snowflakes glistened,
When Santa spoke, the reindeer listened.

"I've had a think, yes I have thunk,
I'm tired of lugging all this junk

Round streets and houses, big and small,
Down chimneys short, and chimneys tall,
To all the children everywhere
Who never really seem to care,
Just play with a toy for half a minute,
Then get all bored, and chuck it – bin it.

So now I've really had enough,
Of giving people all this stuff,
I've had enough, say what you like,
This Christmas, Santa is *on strike!*"

Silence settled with the snow,
As snowflakes tickled reindeer toe,
Was Santa joking? Was he tight?
Did all the reindeer hear him right?

Was something wrong? Was it the weather?
Or something different altogether?

Not even Rudolph, nose a-glow,
Had ever seen him get this low,
Not Donner, Blitzen, nor the rest,
Had ever seen him this depressed,
And they'd seen more than one recession,
But never – ever – this depression.

Santa got down from the sleigh,
"I'm sorry boys," they heard him say,
"And girls, of course, all reindeer friends,
Forgive me if my action ends

Traditions that for years gone by
Have brought a tear to every eye,
Of happiness, not sadness, fear,
But joy, goodwill and Christmas cheer.

I just can't help it, when I see,
Such greed and waste and misery,
When no-one seems to half remember
Just what it means when in December
Christmas comes and we should be
Together, friends and family.

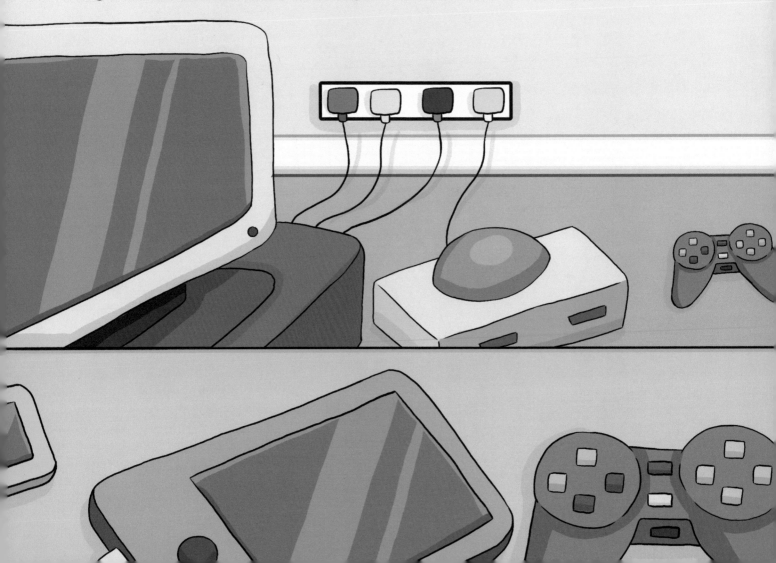

Not full of greed and self-obsessions,
About our latest new possessions.
And even if they are fantastic
All electronic, shiny plastic,
Technology of such precision,
Computer, mobile, television,
They are just things, they're not the reason
To come together Christmas Season."

The reindeer nodded, it was true
That Santa had a point or two,
But what on earth were they to do?

"I'm now on strike," old Santa said,
"So now I'm going off to bed.
This year no Christmas will there be,
For them and us and you and me,
So Donner, Blitzen, Vixen, Dancer,
Dasher, Comet, Cupid, Prancer,
And old friend Rudolph, nose-a-glow,
Tomorrow's our day off, y'know,
So make the most of all the snow!

Be of good cheer and do not worry,
This year, for once, there is no hurry.
So Merry Christmas, everyone,
I'm off to bed, my day is done."

Dancer

Rudolph

The reindeer could not disobey,
And leave alone – just them, and sleigh –
They did not know what else to do,
So settled down to their sleep too.

That Christmas Day, do you know what?
Nobody cared what gifts they got:
They all got nowt – that's not a lot.

But no-one cared – not father, mother,
Boy and girl, and sister, brother,
Because they knew they had each other.

Cupid

On Christmas Night, when Santa woke,
He felt much better, so he spoke.

Prancer

Blitzen

And icicles and snowflakes glistened,
When Santa spoke, all reindeer listened:

"I know it was a bit risqué
To go on strike this Christmas Day,
But Christmas Night is not yet done,
So shake a hoof now, everyone!

My strike is over, now I see
That people know they don't need me.
So don't just stand there getting shivery,
This year's a Boxing Day delivery!

I know the people had to wait,
They'll get their presents one day late.
But now perhaps they'll show less greed,
And only buy just what they need.
And not be so obsessed with money,
Though knowing them that would be funny...

The meaning of Christmas is not us here,
Not me, the sleigh or you reindeer,
The true meaning of Christmas is 'Ho Ho Ho!',
And that means LOVE. Come on, let's go!"

The reindeer nodded, and pulled the sleigh,
Into the night sky far away,
And through the cold and Christmas snow
Came Santa's voice, and he should know:

"Please love each other, have some fun,
And Merry Christmas, everyone!"

Author Profile

Jem Vanston is an author and song writer, perhaps best known for his A CAT CALLED DOG stories. SANTA GOES ON STRIKE is his 6th book. He was born and brought up in Dartford, Kent but now lives in Swansea, South Wales.

Author website: www.vanston.co.uk

Publisher Information

Rowanvale Books provides publishing services to independent authors, writers and poets all over the globe. We deliver a personal, honest and efficient service that allows authors to see their work published, while remaining in control of the process and retaining their creativity. By making publishing services available to authors in a cost-effective and ethical way, we at Rowanvale Books hope to ensure that the local, national and international community benefits from a steady stream of good quality literature.

For more information about us, our authors or our publications, please get in touch.
www.rowanvalebooks.com
info@rowanvalebooks.com

Lightning Source UK Ltd.
Milton Keynes UK
UKIC031024201218
334299UK00003B/55

9 781911 569749